Newspaper Diapers

M. T. Johnson

©2012 TD10 Publishing

ISBN-13: 978-0615723211
ISBN-10: 0615723217

Thanks: Spike Magazine; those who supported this; those who inspired this.

For
Delilah

I try not to use the word optimistic. It's tantamount to saying everything is horrible but it may get better. I prefer to be willing not to judge the now of my life in any way at all and do what I can to simply be the best me I can be. There are a lot of troubles in this world that need transforming. However, a transformed world comes about as a result of a transformed individual, and I'm the individual I must transform. That is my responsibility. So it seems to me I need to be aware of what is happening, but to focus on getting the darkness out of my heart, rather than what is wrong with you... So I can be a part of the answer.

Hubert Selby, Jr.

Physically restrain – *verb*.   In a mental health treatment facility, the act of holding a child to the floor or wall so as to prevent the child from being able to move. Usually done by at least two staff, but possibly eight or more depending on the child's size and strength. The main purpose is one or more of the following: to prevent the child from hurting himself, hurting others, running away, or causing material damage. No tools, weapons, or apparatuses are used in the process.

Because the boys were punching each other, the counselors needed to physically restrain them.

Physical restraint – *noun*. The manifestation of these conditions.

The girl began slashing her wrist, so three counselors placed her in a physical restraint.

I'm a counselor for abused children.

I want to end the cycle.

There's hope.

I'm a counselor for abused children.

I keep them safe so they can grow up to become perpetrators of what fucked them up in the first place.

I want to end the cycle.

I know how to do it.

Kill them all.

There's no such thing as rehabilitation.

Every morning until kindergarten her mother and grandmother forced her to eat oatmeal out of their vaginas.

Three days after she arrived at the facility, a new counselor who didn't know any better served her some and she began screaming and tried to stab him with a plastic knife. While being physically restrained by three therapists, she bashed her head on the floor so many times she passed out. Two cops and three counselors took her to the emergency room on a gurney.

Her imaginary friends taught her the fine art of "cheeking": how to hide psychotropic medication in one's mouth between the gums and cheek.

She's now the most well-behaved kid in the facility, enjoying special privileges such as going to the store by herself and making phone calls without having to ask permission first. It's only a matter of time before she sabotages herself and goes back to square one. Because you can't ever leave square one, can you? The best you can do is hover over it in a perpetual cycle of highs and lows and mediocre plateaus that feel satisfying at first, but soon only function to shine a spotlight on how unstable and hopeless you really are.

When I was an infant, my brother raped me hard enough and often enough to permanently damage my colon, rendering bowel control obsolete. It's common for me to defecate at the lunch table, but the other students are always understanding and never tease.

Pathetic. A complete momma's boy. His biggest fear was physical pain; he knew it and all his friends knew it, too. They'd voted him "Most Likely to Run Away Instead of Defending One of Us" eight years straight. He hated himself.

I can't take it anymore.

He punched his upper cheek several times; a black eye would make him look tough in school the next day. But the potential for success was minimal, considering that the technique he used bore a close resemblance to politely knocking on a door.

He rushed to the mirror the following morning, but there was just a slight yellowish color, visible only upon close inspection. Even mother didn't notice it.

What a fucking loser.

I have a lot of anger towards my parents. I want to get rid of it, but I don't know how. I've tried everything. I criticize people for letting others get them down, yet no one does this more than me. I spend so much time wishing that those who've wronged me would just fucking *suffer*. My past controls me; I can lie and tell you it doesn't, but it does. I'm dominated by all the violations and humiliations I've sought out, all those thrust upon me, and all those I've allowed to go way beyond my limits of what's acceptable. Ignore who you think I am and all the love we both know I'm capable of. I know where I want to be and who I need to be, but I can't get there without your help. Please. This is probably my last chance.

"Hi, I'm your therapist. We'll be meeting after lunch on Tuesdays and Fridays. If you need to get a message to me at any other time, please tell a counselor and they'll send me an email or leave me a voice mail. Try not to come to me every time you have a problem or get upset; you need to try to sort through some problems on your own. I'll be here to help you, of course, but I read in your file that better anger management is one of your goals, and this is a great opportunity to work on it. A case file for new residents always gets sent to all the counselors, so they already know a bit about your family, your destructive behaviors, and the warning signs that you're about to become destructive. I know you've lived in several foster homes and group homes, but as your social worker told you, we have a policy of unconditional love. That means we'll never kick you out of here. It *doesn't* mean you can just do whatever you want. We believe a child needs love and patience to grow and change, and if we kicked you out for doing the same things that brought you here in the first place... that's just not the way you help someone. The other residents and the counselors will help you understand the program better, and they'll teach you all the rules. This is a highly structured program and it'll probably take you a week or two to get acclimated to everything, especially the consequences we have for certain behaviors. Don't be nervous, though. We're all here to help you, and I'm honestly *really* happy you're here."

"Fuck off, bitch."

She grabbed the therapist's ponytail and then yanked it hard enough to separate scalp and skull.

One 10-year-old resident was completely together until an encounter with his mother the previous year.

"Have you ever kissed a girl?"

He shook his head.

"Give your mom a big kiss."

He pecked her cheek.

"Noooooo, I mean a real kiss." She flapped her tongue.

He stared and remained silent.

She pulled his head closer and pushed her tongue past his lips, prodding and playing and dripping in his mouth. He noticed she kept her eyes closed the whole time, and that beads of sweat appeared on her forehead.

After a week of staring in the mirror for hours a day, he needed something to mute the unfamiliar screaming in his head. While out for a walk with his dog Stubby, he gave its leash fierce staccato yanks, painting the pet's eyes red for a week. Stubby's affection toward him remained the same, however, and the stupid dog needed to be taught a lesson.

Let's see how that idiot likes licking my butthole after I poop.

Oh, Stubby. Dear, dear Stubby. The worthless beast wouldn't acquiesce until the boy's pinky was jammed into its urethra, his other hand guiding puppy wuppy's face to his unwiped anus.

"Funtime with Stubby" got boring after a few weeks, so he left the dog alone and began a new activity that involved biting his own hand until the pain compelled release. He named the hand Little Stinker and talked to it and told people it talked to him as well. His teachers noticed and referred him to the school psychologist. Five minutes after their first session ended, he started a fight that culminated in the attempted biting-off of his opponent's nose. The courts determined that his mother was "unable to provide the necessary discipline," so they placed him in a group home for troubled children.

Seven facilities and five foster homes later, he arrived here. On his first night, he got physically restrained for grabbing a female counselor's breast. Just last week, he graced our presence with everything from assaults to bashing his skull on the wall. We physically restrained him every time.

When picking up a phone call from an unknown number, I dreaded hearing her voice; it always caused the feeling of "What *now*?" to consume me.

Once again, she validated my attitude.

Her physically abusive boyfriend found out she'd been a short-term prostitute and was now blackmailing her. He'd gotten hold of a photo that was used to promote her services; these advertisements were necessary because she'd sold herself in Marin County, California, a wealthy suburban area where you can't just stand on a corner to draw customers. The photo he had was of her in lingerie, with the caption, "Make my ass your own personal expressway." He said it would be all over the internet if he couldn't watch her having sex with his best friend.

I had no good advice to offer her — the whole prostitution thing was news to me and caught me off guard. I couldn't stop thinking about the fact that I'd had sex with her after she'd been selling herself and how happy I was that I wore a condom. Her excuse just made it worse.

"It was all the meth I was using at the time."

I always wonder what happened to her. She was a good woman, very intelligent. I hope she's still alive.

The kids hated some of the counselors. The ones who treated them like projects, damaged goods, broken machines in need of repair. The ones who thought that the right advice would save them. The ones who couldn't separate the kids from the abuse they'd suffered. The ones on power trips.

The kids loved and protected some of the counselors. The ones who asked genuine questions. The ones who listened. The ones who encouraged their actual interests, not the interests they were supposed to have. The ones who didn't take their crap, who told them to shut up when they needed to shut up. The ones who treated them like peers. Like friends. Like people.

Those kids could spot the real thing better than you'll ever be able to.

At family gatherings my father made it his mission to keep me on a very short leash; he'd monitor my every move, and then pounce when I did anything that even slightly deviated from his image of how a perfect daughter should behave. It was like he thrived on punishing me, making me feel small in front of others. Now that I think about it, he did it in front of my friends, too. Being in his presence has always made me feel uncomfortable. And despite pleas and promises, he's never really changed; he's just been forced to adapt to me being an adult. What a dick.

I think I was sexually abused as a small child, but I have no conscious memory of it, and no suspects.

Vacations always brought out the worst in one of my favorite kids at the facility. It was like she couldn't handle all the positivity. Amusement parks, forget about it. She once trashed a hotel room after a day of roller coasters and giggles. During the destruction, she ate a light bulb. The hospital instructed her to defecate into a bowl for two weeks to make sure there was no internal damage; some unlucky counselor had to sift through the shit, looking for blood or anything else of interest. On day three, a screw appeared.

"I ate that a few weeks ago, I swear! I haven't hurt myself since the hotel. You gotta believe me!"

The kids who'd behaved for the entire month were rewarded with a counselor-escorted camping trip. She managed to avoid any outbursts and self-harm incidents during the specified period, and was thus allowed to attend. On the second night, she started grunting and screaming due to no obvious external stimuli. A therapist tried to redirect her negative energy to a conversation about horses. Nice try.

"If I had one of my weapons with me, I'd kill you."

Silence.

"I'm not joking."

He just stared at her. "I believe you."

Moments later, she lunged at him teeth-first and successfully latched onto his hand. To the rescue were four counselors who physically restrained her for three and a half hours.

Back at the facility the next evening, she was

calm and kept apologizing for the eight-minute bite* she'd inflicted on her favorite therapist.

> *All useful teeth-removal tactics were prohibited due to being potentially injurious to the child. You essentially had to let the kids bite you until they felt like releasing.*

Nerve damage in the soft webbing between the man's index finger and thumb rendered him unable to work for six weeks. The lingering hand twitch helps him reminisce about the camping trip.

He still works at the facility.

"You're an idiot!"

Thanks Mom.

"You know what I say? Kill all the Iraqis!"

Thanks Dad.

It's good to have some guilt and regret to carry with you. Channel self-contempt and self-loathing into stronger values, thoughts, and behavior.

Bullshit. Your guilt and regret just weigh you down. Cast them aside. Be who you want to be. Be yourself.

From the time my boyfriend was born, his parents argued in front of him and his siblings all the time. They insulted each other, shouted threats, and made remarks to the kids about what a loser their spouse was. *Not once* did either one apologize with this same audience present.

My boyfriend and his siblings were affected in various ways: he both voluntarily and involuntarily defecated in his pants almost every day from ages 3 to 17; his younger sister's always angry and has stress-induced irritable bowel syndrome; and his younger brother screams in his sleep several times a week and has no idea how to take care of his basic hygiene needs. All three of them have serious emotional issues and a complete inability to be part of a healthy relationship.

"Shut up pig! Shut up pig! Shut up pig!"

She was having her nightly exclamation-inducing nightmare. Before entering her bedroom to wake her, I asked my co-worker to keep an eye on me; male counselors weren't allowed to enter a female resident's room without another counselor monitoring. False allegations of sexual misconduct were common. Of course, sometimes they were true. Like when a resident accused my former co-worker of impregnating and then trying to abort her with a wire hanger. That one was true. Dudes like that ruined it for the rest of us male counselors, 99 percent of whom aren't death-penalty-deserving maggots.

"Shut up pig!"

I woke her up and asked what she was dreaming about.

"My parents."

I don't know why I even bothered anymore—it was the same answer every night.

I love porn. (Obviously nothing with children or animals! Who do you think I am anyway?) A close-up of an anus after it's been penetrated by a huge penis or foreign object and then spread wide for the camera divides most viewers into two categories: those wanting to replicate the act, and those who cringe and are ready to vomit. But I just feel curious and really sympathetic for the anus's owner. Women's bodies are constantly on my mind, and I spend most of my free time imagining what every foxy lady's tushy looks and smells and tastes like.

Come on baby, just pull your pants down slow. Let me put my nose in your ass crack and smell it. The more heat and sweat, the better the fragrance. You know what I'm talking about. *Everyone's* interested in licking someone's asshole and having theirs licked, too. It feels good, don't lie. Ask your lover to shave around the hole (and the cheeks, if necessary, or if that's what you prefer) and just dig in. It's soft and tight and smells and tastes great. Yes, it does! I've never pictured an anus shitting or farting when I'm munching on one. I think the people who *do* picture that are the oddballs, not me.

Her brother's puppy always bit and scratched her for no damn reason and she hated it. After learning that dogs have sensitive ears, she developed a strategy to deal with the attacks: If she was minding her own business and that little bastard jumped up and clawed her, she'd retaliate by clutching its skull and shrieking in its ear. The poor guy always tried in vain to extract his head from her grip, but she could never tell if the shrieks were painful or merely annoying. Slathering her sphincter with whipped cream for the dog to lick off probably crossed the line she'd drawn between acceptable retaliation and pure exploitation.

"I loved him so much. He was one of the best friends I ever had."

Recalling his psychology textbook's discussion of the usefulness of physical contact when intimate personal details are revealed, the counselor gave her a hug and encouraged her to continue crying until she felt better. Citing an illness in the family, he quit a week later.*

> * An absurdly large percentage of counselors who quit in the first couple months on the job happened to have mothers "get sick"; it was easier to lie than admit you couldn't handle the job.

He now works as a claims adjuster and things are a lot easier. Thanks for coming. Next!

Verbal abuse is just as harmful as physical abuse, and often more difficult to heal from.

She was lying in bed feigning an attempt at falling asleep, angry at her therapist and in need of attention more than slumber.

Inhale.

Exhale; with each exhalation, she simultaneously whispered "die."

Inhale.

"Die."

Inhale.

"Die."

Inhale.

"Die."

The counselor sitting at her bedroom door just ignored her and continued reading his book; she always pulled stunts like this at bedtime and one false move might cause her to savagely attack.

She's now a mother of three and proudly displays the self-inflicted scars decorating her arms.

I grew up saying nigger, spick, chink, gook, jewbag, dyke, homo, fag, queer... plenty more, I'm sure. I wish someone had put me in my place long before you did.

This is why I want to do something great with my life. Don't you get it? I was raised to be nothing. Mediocre, at best. I know I'm capable of so much more, yet I feel completely unable to achieve it.

8 AM. He stood in the shower masturbating, knowing he was about to do something special, something the counselors would still be talking about years later. He was really smart and effective in the art of annoying, repulsing, and humiliating them. They were just thankful he wasn't violent.

When his shower hit the 20-minute mark, everyone knew trouble was brewing and began to hassle him by asking what he was doing, when he was coming out, and reminding him of all he had to be proud of. They'd recited this pointless spiel many times before.

This would be a three-round fight.

DING!

The bell rang to start Round 1. He ejaculated on a blank piece of paper, folded it in half, and slid it under the door, requesting that his most hated female counselor read "this list of demands." She opened it and—before comprehending why there was nothing to read—used her semen-coated finger to scratch her itchy eye. DING! That's the end of Round 1.

Three more counselors gathered outside the shower door to assist, bringing the total to six.

DING!

He squatted and defecated on the floor, then spread the fresh pile on his entire body, making sure to thoroughly coat his biceps, calves, and forearms (the parts they'd have to hold during the inevitable physical restraint). DING! That's the end of Round 2.

He opened the door and stared at his eager

audience, his expression appearing more nonchalant than menacing.

DING!

When he refused to walk to the seclusion room, the counselors physically restrained him on the floor. After the initial shock and disgust wore off, some of them began laughing and joking about the situation. The feces soon hardened, causing it to flake and crumble. One counselor flicked a shit ball at his co-worker; it landed in her ear. DING!

The night counselors arrived several hours later. Two powerful fans had done nothing to dispel the odor, so everyone immediately asked why the whole place smelled like a toilet.

"You-know-who spread feces all over himself and was restrained for a couple hours."

"Oh."

When I was eight, I was playing with my dolls in my mother's bedroom and she walked out of the bathroom topless.

"Do you want to pretend to breastfeed? It's been so long."

I nodded.

It was the first week of 7th grade.

I followed her out of class and down the hall, all
the while mocking her obesity with various
names and insults.

She just ignored me.

I'm sure she'd mastered that art years before.

An older student threw me up against the wall.

"If you ever make fun of someone because of their
weight again, I'll *kill* you."

Any usefulness found in the platitudes my parents
recited was negated by the way they actually
lived.

But the second that threat hit my powers of consid-
eration, I recognized its wisdom.

I have yet to disobey the order.

I'm thankful I've never been in a fight, because I hold a grudge like you wouldn't believe. It wouldn't even matter if I won or not—I'd make it my life's mission to ensure suffering. I'm sick in the head. I've been having flashbacks of what you all did to me, and the courage I've always known I had is just now rearing its head. For my entire life, I've dreaded physical confrontation. And now, the pendulum has swung to the other side, maybe a bit too far. I don't necessarily *want* a fight, but I'm not about to run from one either.

"I didn't like her very much. She was a nice person and had good taste in music, but she was annoying and made stupid jokes. Her breasts were nothing special, and her ass—when not bent over, just hanging there—was almost shockingly flabby for such a petite chick. It wasn't wide, just loooong and droopy. But when she was on all fours, letting me do my thing, it suddenly morphed into quite the tush. The first time I licked her asshole, she expressed the usual concerns: 'I've never had that done before…I don't know…Do you really *like* that?' Soon, though, she was craving it. They all do. 'It's really difficult to make me come.' When I licked her tight little booty-hole while rubbing her clit with my thumb she came right away. She was on all fours and I was kneeling on the bed, putting my face in perfect position to devour her beautiful coochie. Is there anything yummier? I just bury my face in there. I wrap my arms around the thighs, each fitting perfectly in the crook of an elbow, and my hands meet anywhere between the lower and middle part of her back. If she's not in my favorite position, where her lower back is pushed down and her ass is pushed up, I apply a little pressure until there's a perfect arch. Back goes down, butt goes up. Hahaha. I then run my tongue from the top of her clit to the top of her ass crack—touching, tasting, and smelling everything in between—and then back down again. Up and down, up and down. If you play your cards right, her asshole will start to peek open just a little. You don't need to push your tongue inside to achieve this; the steady, soft rhythm will take care of it. Soon enough. And as you drag your tongue over her pucker, it'll make a sound that has less pop than a popping sound and more crackle than a crackling sound. Seeing a gorgeous hole opening a bit, right in front of my face, all because I'm taking good care of it.... I gotta admit it's one of my greatest pleasures in life. I remember one time she took her clothes off and stood there in just her bra and panties. I was sitting on a chair and she was standing, just offering herself to me. I turned her around, pulled the thong out of her crack, and spread her flabby cheeks apart a little bit with my thumbs. It was a warm evening, so when I went to get a quick whiff-'n-taste I could smell a little sweat. She was a classy woman. I'll give her that much."

I told her I got the point and that she shouldn't have been talking after lights out anyway. She stopped rambling and fell asleep a minute later. I didn't even bother to document her monologue; did all my co-workers *really* need a recap?

Your whole life is a lie.

Your family's not a family.

Never was, never will be.

Just a group of people with a complete inability to respect and relate to one other.

A couple of emotionally unstable American psychos got together and produced offspring to occupy all the empty space in their fucked up lives.

"Produced" being the key word here, my man.

You guys were just products, items to them.

They were able to assert control for only so long before it all blew up.

The present has been reduced to romanticizing the past, telling the same goddamn stories over and over, the rest of the time spent destroying themselves and each other.

All they wanted was to be great parents who raised perfect little children.

They failed.

Their dreams crumbled.

They hate you for exposing the true reality of the family.

Move on, my friend.

They're not worth it.

Three girls started a riot. You resisted as long as you could before planting a lunging bite on a man 45 minutes into day one of his new job. Nice one; it really hurt. Some of my co-workers pried you off the leg after only a minute. My friend lost her glasses, which you grabbed and broke. How you got the lens in your mouth so quickly still amazes me.

"Make good decisions!"

"Keep yourself safe, sweetie!"

"You know what you need to do!"

We sounded like a bunch of idiots reciting the *How To Reprogram A Horrifically-Abused Child in 15 Easy Steps* handbook.

Why'd you decide to eat the glass, anyway? Was it the rush of the chaos? Were you having flashbacks of your aunt sucking your nipples? Wait wait, I know—you were thinking about the time your mother traded you (just for a night) to a horny friend for a bag of crystal meth! Am I right? Well, what matters is that you chomped on the glass, despite all the pleading and all the therapeutic interventions being employed. As blood trickled down your chin, I actually felt really bad for you. But when you swallowed the shards, I don't know. That might have pushed my patience over the edge. I'd never seen you cry so much, and I'd seen a *lot* of tears fall from your eyes. You stopped struggling with me and the five other counselors, and we let you wash your face before the paramedics took you to the hospital. Were you shocked when the doctor said you had a perforated

colon and needed surgery? Did you even understand what the woman was talking about?

On my eighth birthday, some neighbors and I were playing football in the park next to my house. After the game, with apparently nothing better to do, the older boys—some of whom were my friends—encouraged three younger boys—also my friends—to pick a fight with me. As if they knew the best way to embarrass me in that moment, they complied and pushed me to the ground. Everyone laughed. I wasn't injured, but I still ran home crying. It was one of those situations we all fantasize about: You shrug off their chuckles, stand tall, and prove your worth. But in real life it rarely happens that way, and like me, you get stuck with a painful memory you can't ever forget.

I bet all those sacks of shit still live in the same town, still gathering at the local bars to reminisce about their heydays (before the ugly wives, shitty jobs, and realizations that their lives amounted to nothing). You motherfuckers blew it.

You thought I'd cheated on you.

I hadn't.

I went to your apartment to try to resolve things and comfort you.

You answered the door drunk and knife-wielding.

I was terrified.

You sliced your stomach.

I started crying.

To humiliate me and relieve some of your anger, you slapped my head a few times.

All of this was to make sure I would never want you back.

Or want you in my life in *any* capacity.

It worked.

Thanks for all you taught me.

I don't hate you at all.

It just has to be this way.

Her father was a bigoted, self-described victim of everything from affirmative action to high taxes, a prototypical baby boomer who lapped up the American Dream, poisoned the planet through action or inaction, pleaded ignorance and occasional concern, and then became defensive and blameless. The Dream requires a perfect family, so he abandoned his daughter from a previous marriage (he wasn't afraid to make sacrifices — what-a-guy). A pathological liar who never took responsibility for his problems, he made a career out of severing relationships, self-sabotage, and blaming, blaming, blaming.

But on a day-to-day basis, he was a decent guy who usually treated people well. Coaching children's sports always brought out the best in him. He was a perfect coach who encouraged hard work and cooperation and treated everyone fairly. The stupid kids, the unathletic kids, the kids of a race not his own — all were given love and respect.

"I know he does his best. I just wish he didn't hate himself so much."

Your chances for reconciliation are fading fast. It's now or never.

He prayed for acne so people would know he was going through puberty and becoming a man. Swimming in gym class was a nightmare; while some classmates could grow beards, even his armpits were bald. He considered gluing on some dog hair, but figured the potential sight of it floating in the pool would only compound the ridicule quotient.

His friends lacked the social currency he craved, didn't inject the kind of confidence he wanted and needed. If he tumbled down some stairs and broke an arm, he could try to get all the popular kids to sign his cast, even the hot girls; a cast full of signatures would show his friends that he was clearly much cooler than they realized, that he was an unappreciated star.

The plan was to invite everyone to a party at his house, even the popular kids he'd never met, the ones who definitely didn't know his name or that he even attended their school. When they heard the songs he'd chosen to play — an eclectic mix that showed his diverse taste in everything from Public Enemy to Led Zeppelin — they would understand that he'd been unfairly excluded from their ranks, that he needed to be saved from the losers he was forced to call friends.

He didn't realize how amazing his real friends actually were.

It took me years to understand what true loyalty is, how to show it, and why it's important. What a shame. I'm nobody's best friend and I need to face up to that and own it and accept it. I was a gossiping, unfaithful friend for so long and this is what I get.

The story appeared in all the local newspapers: A 12-year-old boy had witnessed his mother's murder at the hands of his longtime molester. More specifically, he'd seen his mother's boyfriend shoot her nineteen times.

When they found out the boy would be living in their facility, some of the counselors felt like a celebrity was coming, and told their friends and family.

"That boy who was in the news a couple weeks ago, remember?! I'm gonna be working with him!"

The excitement disappeared shortly after his arrival.

His case file noted frequent, extreme panic attacks, attributed to posttraumatic stress disorder. Within weeks, the counselors could predict when one was about to occur; hushed rhetorical questions about the murder almost guaranteed one. *How could you shoot someone nineteen times?"*

The Future Rapist. That's what some of the counselors called him behind his back. Writing in his journal usually kept him occupied, but his true passion in life was exposing his penis to females of all ages. He once summoned a counselor to his bedroom by requesting help with his painting, and when she walked in he was on all fours with a paintbrush lodged in his anus. She hurried away to ask for assistance from her co-workers, but by the time everyone got to his room he'd pulled up his pants and adamantly denied any knowledge of the incident. They confiscated his journal and told him his special privileges would be curtailed for the rest of the week.

I know all the bad stuff I've done. How could I forget? I know I've hurt dogs, friends, relatives. I know I've stood by like a coward while those close to me were humiliated or attacked. I hate myself. Let it be known.

His mother's girlfriend used to molest him every night, so he started urinating in his pajamas to make himself less desirable. He's a resident at our facility now, away from the abuse, but he involuntarily wets the bed most nights; his body internalized the fear, and continues to protect him even when there's no abuse he needs protecting from.

We need to look closer. Somewhere in the world there's a kid pissing for protection right this moment. In Siem Reap, a man's cock is bruising the esophagus of a four-year-old prostitute he's holding by the back of the neck. Something similar is probably going on in your town as well.

This mess is unsustainable. We need to expose reality and fix it. And don't tell me I'm being heavy-handed — the time for subtleties and patience has long expired.

"I could orchestrate anything. No one has more charisma or willpower than me. You're so lucky I'm a good person. If I decided to cross the line that I'm constantly towing, I could be the next Pol Pot or Joseph Kony. Seriously. I could lead a country to hell. You're all fortunate I don't wanna do that, because I care about people and I'm a good person. But I do love revenge. I can zero in on the best way to respond to betrayal or disrespect and carry it out without a second thought. I don't care who it hurts and what the consequences are. So many people are so lucky I don't have the power I wish I had."

At 3 AM, she woke up and urinated in the empty soda bottle on her desk. The nightly ritual. Sometimes, if she didn't feel like aiming, it was her hamper instead. The overnight counselors couldn't figure out the rationale; they were just thankful she never decided to hurl a piss bottle at them in the middle of the night as they watched *The Golden Girls*.

Every morning, two counselors inspected her room to make sure she'd cleaned and organized everything according to the facility's rules. Inevitably, they'd find the bottle and smell the urine wafting from her hamper.

"I didn't do it."

Same statement every day: always curt, always coupled with a blank expression, always exuding sincerity.

How I'll reach my goals

1. Stop trying to control everything.

2. Stop looking for reasons or excuses to get angry.

3. Stop making a current boyfriend pay for the mistakes of others.

4. Stop watching porn. Completely. It probably makes me not appreciate the sexual connection between my boyfriend and me.

5. Have a calm and patient attitude with the people I love.

6. Establish clear, strong boundaries. That way I won't have to live in fear of being disrespected by inappropriate comments and questions.

7. Always do what I need to do for myself so I'm emotionally healthier in all facets of life.

The little girl had a lazy eye. There was definitely something wrong with her. She wasn't retarded, just slow or mentally challenged in some way. It was almost like she was always in a deep sleep, the kind where your drooling wakes you up, and no matter how many times you close your mouth, it happens again and again. And she *did* drool a lot.

I can't say she was annoying me because she pretty much just *sat* there. Didn't cry, whine, or bother anyone. But she just fucking irritated me and I couldn't take it anymore. I reached over and pinched her hand hard enough to make any other 5-year-old at least say "ouch." I honestly had no good reason to do this. Maybe it was because she was an easy target. She didn't cry or glance my way. It was as if she didn't even notice, like she was in a deep, drooling sleep.

When my mother went to prison, my father started depending on me and leaning on me for emotional support. It just got worse and worse as time wore on. I realize that I wasn't nearly as supportive during that period as I could have been, but his behavior was still inexcusable and scarring and downright wrong. What a terrible part of my life. Yeah, I know I'm fortunate to have all I have, but emotional abuse really does a number on you. It threw me right into the arms of a toxic, vicious relationship, one in which I sought solace, a place to hide. That experience gave me even more issues, ones I have yet to recover from.

My father complained to me too much and put a ton of pressure on me. He would call me often when I was at my boyfriend's house, didn't respect my adulthood, and was irrational and crazy in so many different ways. I think that whole experience made me really leery of intimacy, because it made me think all men are needy and controlling.

For my entire life, my father has made negative comments to and about my mother in front of my siblings and me. I have such a despicable model for relationships. I equate all my past ones with negativity and therefore always enter a new one with a great deal of pessimism. I don't know if it's a self-fulfilling prophecy or not, but I have yet to be part of a healthy relationship.

I think if I were more confident about my place in life, I'd attract, and be attracted to, men who are healthier and more responsible. I'm sick of all the goddamn issues. I don't want to be the savior any-more.

A year after we broke up, her crack-addict mother
died drunk driving.

I had to hide my excitement as she told me.

One less piece of shit in the world.

Two years later, her racist, child-beating father died
of a stroke.

I laughed when I read the news in the paper.

Two less pieces of shit in the world.

I understand you so much better than I did a few years ago. Remember all those nights when you'd writhe on your bed in complete emotional agony? You'd sob and plead for a hug, but I always refused and said, "It's something you need to work out on your own." Remember twice catching me rolling my eyes? I'm sorry. Damn, I'm *so* sorry. I don't know why it took me so long to grasp how terrified you were, and how horribly I treated you. I guess I had to experience days and nights filled with my own sobs and pleas for a hug. But I was lucky enough to have someone help me in the ways I should have helped you. I wish I'd treated you like a person instead of like a lost-cause abused kid. I always hated when other counselors did that, yet I see now that I was no better than them. The more I reflect on my life, the more I come to despise myself. I can do better, and I promise you I will.

Two pencils she'd smuggled from The Shared Space* were calling her name. They were hidden in her stuffed turtle, next to the screws and glass.

* *The Shared Space was where the residents were expected to socialize and enjoy life. There was a TV, a table, and some couches. One of the counselors had hung paintings on the wall to make it feel more like home; it didn't work at all.*

In plain view of an onlooking male counselor, she extracted one of the pencils and tucked it in her waistband. The man was paying attention and doing his best, but monitoring teenagers—trying to ensure that they don't hurt themselves or each other—gets monotonous and predictable like any other job; boredom sets in, routines develop, mistakes happen.

In class an hour later, she asked to be excused to use the restroom. A recent incident** had earned her additional supervision, even when on the toilet; this entailed leaving the door open a few inches and a counselor standing directly outside (out of view), enabling unbroken communication.

** *Three days prior, she'd used up an entire asthma inhaler in under a minute and was sent to the emergency room with chest pains. During the visit, she managed to swipe a small bottle of blood pressure medication.*

She sat on the toilet, released the pencil she'd

somehow transferred from waistband to rectum, and displaying only the slight grimace that accompanies minor defecation discomfort, buried it in a recent self-inflicted gash on the inside of her forearm.

Her wound dripped on the table during dinner, resulting in another visit to the emergency room.

At the facility an hour later, she confessed to her favorite counselor that she'd stolen the blood pressure medication the previous visit and had been hiding it deep inside her vagina. After dislodging it in the restroom, she placed the warm bottle in his gloved hand.

"Newspaper Diapers"
(sung to the tune of "This Little Light Of Mine")

Born inside a crack house

No diapers to be found

Her parents had to use

Old newspapers instead

She's seventeen and still

Pisses the bed

Pisses the bed

Pisses the bed

Pisses the bed

In my dream last night, I confronted my father about all the destruction he and my mother wreaked upon me. You came along for support. Only, in the dream, you were your younger self, before the drugs and the prostitution. You waited for me to say what I needed to say, displaying the sexy patience you've always had. Or at least you had it when I knew you, when you were young and hopeful and full of so much potential to be whoever you wanted to be, a brief window of time that resided between all the childhood abuse you suffered and all the adulthood abuse you'd seek and accept. I still feel guilty, like if I hadn't ended our relationship, instead of a window it would have been a door. I could have helped you unlock it, coaxed you to walk through, and then locked it behind you so you'd never be able to return to the shit. Sometimes I wonder if your life would have turned out differently if I'd helped you more when I knew you, so long ago, before the drugs and the prostitution.

SMACK!

The dog's thigh was muscular, yet soft enough to satisfy my urge to hear a good slap. My teeth were clenched as I heard a steady stream of insults moshing in my brain. "You stupid pussy, fight back." I might have actually said that one.

I beat my beautiful dog to relieve the anger I felt toward my parents. There, I said it. Usually in the evening, a few times a week, for I don't know how long. A year? It's better that I can't really remember certain periods of my life; my history prior to a certain point is colored with all sorts of deplorable acts.

I didn't understand my need to fight with the dog, nor that it *was* a need.

These memories surface way too often. The ability to completely forgive oneself is a myth for most of us.

When she was four, the boy next door raped her. Throughout her teens and early twenties a lot of men had tried to win her love. Some had seemingly succeeded, but it was pure illusion: She'd pretend to let them in her heart, wait until they got confident about the relationship, cheat on them, and then rescind her past declarations of love.

"There are different kinds of love, you know? What I meant to say was that I really care about you and like you a lot."

It wasn't a choice — she *needed* to treat men like garbage. My theory is that she was incapable of loving a man because of how much she hated her body. I mean, she wouldn't even take off her bra during sex, and she was so damn self-conscious about her vaginal aroma.

And beware, all you prospective suitors: If your body's in good shape, it'll make her hate hers even more. Your gym membership will blow up right in your face!

There was a counselor from Cambodia, a woman whose family—the few who weren't executed or starved to death—had fled to the U.S. during the reign of the Khmer Rouge. She'd survived the most harrowing of circumstances and was now trying to help teenagers get their lives straightened out.

One evening after dinner, she asked a usually calm but sometimes extremely violent resident to turn his music down; the boy responded to her polite request by completely smashing her face with a sucker punch to the jaw. Facial reconstructive surgery followed hours later.

She never returned to work.

I've been picking and biting my nails since I was a child. What probably started out as a nervous habit evolved into a way to punish myself. I chomp until one or more hangnails are present, "accidentally" induce bleeding by yanking them out with my teeth, get angry and disappointed with my behavior, and then make a vow to myself: *I'll-never-do-it-again, I'll-never-do-it-again, this was definitely the last time.*

It's just like when I watch porn. The stuff hasn't actually turned me on in years. It long ago became a drug, a way to zone out and be in total control and not think about anything, a way to make the minutes zoom by. Moments after my orgasm, I get angry that I wasted so much time, even though whatever I could have been doing instead wouldn't have been nearly as gratifying. I've never rationalized anything as much as watching porn.

It'll make me appreciate my partner more.

I just really admire the human body.

It helps me stay one hundred percent faithful.

I'll learn more about human sexuality and new positions and moves to try in bed.

I've said them all to myself. But overall, porn hasn't been detrimental to my life or made me a worse person. Despite being a source of momentary depression now and then, it's probably helped me stay focused.

With the exception of growing breasts, it was like she never advanced past the age of 6. A really sweet girl with limited social skills, it was almost impossible for her to stay focused in a conversation for more than a minute, and she constantly made jokes at inappropriate times. A counselor would be giving her a pep-talk, trying to impart words of wisdom, and just as he was finding his groove, she'd smile and say something like, "Your eyebrows are weird." This would completely interrupt his flow, thus preventing him from being able to save the world—one young person at a time—by giving hope and perspective and passing on all the wisdom he'd gained when attaining his psychology or sociology degree.*

> * *Most of the counselors lacked sufficient credibility to give any advice that held much weight. Many had serious emotional issues and were playing the age-old game of trying to fix everyone else's problems; it's a lot easier to tell rape victims how to move past their trauma than it is cast out your own demons.*

Her mother used heroin before, during, and after the pregnancy, so everyone pitied her for being somewhat doomed from conception. Her father was even worse, beating the hell out of her a few times a week and subjecting her to all kinds of sick shit. She bragged about progressing to a pain and humiliation threshold that allowed her, at age nine, to not cry as he shoved her head into a feces-filled toilet and then insisted she go to bed without a shower. Despite enduring his ceaseless abuse, she seemed most devastated and damaged by an incident with her uncle.

Age 10. Woken up by the placement of her hand in his pants. No tears or scowls, just complete astonishment at what was transpiring. 11 minutes. Him guiding her little hand on his penis until he ejaculated on her shirt (pink with three red balloons and a caption that said "Smiley Day"). Sliding his middle finger into her vagina. Walking away without a word.

During her intake interview, one of the therapists encouraged her to discuss the minutia of her background, so as to establish "a relationship of familiarity and transparency from the get-go." Able to revisit the madness with what resembled complete apathy, like she was explaining a homework assignment, everything changed when the incident with her uncle took center stage. As one therapist documented, "The story was told entirely in third person, yet she seemed to be reliving the molestation while recounting the incident."

She lived at the facility for a few years, made little if any progress, and then got transitioned to an adult facility shortly after her 18th birthday.

I wish I could have done more to help you. I think of you often, and I hope you're safe, wherever you are.

"I wanna change myself. I'm sick of coming up short on self-care. I'm positive I can change because I truly feel I can accomplish anything I'm passionate about. I need to get more in touch with who I really am and finally figure out what I'm going to do for a career. I think when I do, I'll like my life more and be more proactive with taking care of myself and building a good life. I won't be as weighed down by guilt and depression, and my reactions will be more appropriate and level-headed. I wanna have a better, healthier, happier life, and I'm committed to making it happen. I think my life is a lot unhealthier than it appears to be—not just to other people, but to myself as well."

<u>Part 1: Touch your rectum. You'll be surprised how</u>
<u>squishy it is.</u>

(THIS ONE'S ABOUT YOU.) In 3rd grade, he began holding in his feces so he could prolong the pleasure of pre-defecation rectal pressure. That orgasmic feeling when release is imminent and the hole becomes softer, more malleable, like it's opening and crooning a lush ballad. For you. Only you. Who else could hear it, or even want to hear it? "That's *my* hiney-hole, buddy, cover your ears. It's singing to ME, not YOU. It's my private concert, you greedy son of a bitch. If you play your cards right (you know what I mean... hold your shit in just the perfect way to make YOUR butthole sing to you), pretty soon you'll be hearing the same sweet sphincter songs. And hey, if my advice works, you should come back and show me some appreciation. Lovely ladies, you can let me see your ass and give it a little kiss and sniff. And gentlemen, you can do some yardwork around my house."

He'd sit on the ground and pull his knees up to his chest, a delightful position that made his body eager to expel and the anal sensations all the more intense. It took skill to find the optimum balance of control, pleasure, and timing.

He graduated to putting his index finger far enough inside to touch his rectum. Interestingly enough, he never inserted any objects other than a pen a few times and a drumstick once (the kind for playing music, not a chicken leg you freak!). But there was definitely no malice involved. Just pure curiosity. Whenever his finger scraped against the ready-to-get-going rectal content, he'd observe that though it didn't quite have the anger of a caged animal, it was definitely salivating at the thought of release.

Part 2: Evolution, maturation, ointment application

I gave myself hemorrhoids of the internal and external variety. I forced and forced and forced until the bleeding, the shitting-glass sensation, and the bulging, grape-sized veins adorning the entrance/exit became unbearable. I've also had anal fissures, one of which bled like a motherfucker and took over a year to heal.

In order to feel whole, like ME, I must always have:

1. A physical malady.
2. One or more enemies — abstract or corporeal — in my immediate surroundings.
3. An excuse for why I'm not living my life fully.
4. Justification for my indiscretions.

On her first day at the facility, one of my favorite residents barely engaged with the counselor inquiring about her hobbies. After much prodding, she finally admitted that she loved music and art and black clothes and nose piercings.

"I used to be the singer in a heavy metal band." And while grinning, "I'm a screamer."

During math class the next afternoon, she had flashbacks of her brother's beatings and began violently clawing her arms. While being physically restrained she let out several deafening screams. The questioning counselor was there, and he immediately recalled the previous day's quip.

"I'm a screamer."

Grin.

Some of my goals

- To let myself accept love.

- To become more trustworthy if and when trust is earned.

- To treat my girlfriend like an equal and a friend.

- To be loving and affectionate more often.

- To not make my girlfriend pay for ex-girlfriends' indiscretions.

Why I want and need to change

- There's too much arguing in my relationships.

- I feel horrible when I treat my girlfriend poorly.

- Being suspicious of dishonesty is all-consuming.

- I feel depressed and down on myself when I'm in a relationship.

- Making someone I love cry feels terrible. I hate it when I do that.

Potential rewards and benefits

- A relationship that would enhance my life rather

than detract from it.

- Feeling trust for a woman would be liberating.

- Much more time and energy for good things instead of constantly fighting and making up.

- Being in a consistently positive relationship for the first time.

- Finally *feeling* like my girlfriend is one of my best friends instead of just *thinking* it.

- I would like my life more and would feel more balanced and healthy.

My fears

- If women aren't the enemy anymore, will I still be me? Will I keep my identity?

- I don't know if I can handle trusting my girlfriend as much as I want to.

- Will I be able to truly separate ex-girlfriends' transgressions from the present?

- Will I like myself if I'm in a good relationship for a long time?

- When my ability to attract different women is no longer a prime motivator for excellence, will I be less driven to succeed?

(THIS ONE'S ABOUT ME.) She hurt herself to force into the background the pain she felt every second of every day. Like when she needed to forget the sensation of her father's three motor-oil-lubed fingers in her anus, or the bite marks he left on her shoulder. Her favorite kind of pain was that which lingered, like each time she sat down after wiping her anus until it swelled and bled way more than you'd expect from such a tiny organ. Or the constant pain she felt after accidentally swallowing glass while teaching herself how to hide shards in the back of her mouth. The pain filled the part of her that's so numb and hollow, filled it with something she could actually *feel*, something that reminded her she's alive.

Many had showed her love and care and affection, gave her the loyalty and dedication they felt she deserved—that she *did* deserve. But when you try to love a damaged soul, you rarely get the positive outcome you might expect. It's the same story with boyfriends and girlfriends: "She's been abused and disrespected so much for so long, so when she experiences *true* love and respect, she'll love me that much more. She must be completely fed up with mistreatment. My wonderful support and unconditional care will just hook her in. She'll never leave me." Bullshit. Here was a girl who had no idea how to be loved and never wasted a golden opportunity to sabotage a relationship. You're the same way.

Damn, I'd waited so many years, suffered through so many insane hoes, all to find one who'd lick my asshole. My time had finally come. It was this cute chick, not beautiful, but certainly cute enough. She could deep throat and her nipples smelled like silly putty.

While giving me a blow job on our second date, she flicked her tongue on my asshole for just a second. I think she was trying to gauge my response; if only she'd heard the hallelujahs frolicking between my ears.

On our next date, I was standing next to the bed and she was taking my entire dick down her throat. I'm fairly large for a non-porn star, so this really impressed me. Could it be that the first to deep throat my cock would also be the first to toss my salad? This was all way too much for even *my* filthy mind to grasp. Suddenly, without a word or even a change of expression,* she flipped over, lay on her back, arched herself up in a way that must have become uncomfortable in the ensuing minutes, and began licking my asshole. I put one hand under her chin and one on her breast, before quickly realizing that one of them would be better served stroking my dick, spitting on it frequently to maintain lubrication.

That's not entirely accurate. Her face remained in the same state of enjoyment and desire, but she gained a subtle look that told me she had a new mission and was determined to succeed.

She ended things the following year. Though

she was a cool woman and we had some great times together, the only thing I ever missed about her was her insatiable appetite for my ass.

My friend didn't get circumcised until he was eight. The procedure was botched, blood flowed, and he's been crazy ever since. A slew of medications has only served to stabilize his instability. Success is now measured by how often he talks to himself on any given day. While visiting him at the facility last week, our conversation about my husband ended when he abruptly started discussing his family.

"I'm thankful my parents didn't beat me. If they had—even *once*—I know I'd have slit their throats while they were sleeping and watched them bleed to death while I stood motionless waiting for the police to arrive, and when I justified the executions they'd take me to a home for twisted children. Thanks, Mommy and Daddy, for not beating me, because I'd be a nightmare if you had, one of the worst monsters the world's ever seen. I'm crazy and I know it."

I tried to redirect him to a more positive topic, but that rarely works; you usually just have to let the rambling run its course.

"My father's a good guy. I know you don't like him because he drinks a lot and one time when he was drunk he squeezed the back of my neck and threw me to the ground and because he encouraged me to be someone I'm not so it fell more in line with his hopes for me. But he's a great father and you just need to give the man a chance."

For years I wanted a girlfriend who was really possessive and couldn't live without me.

If we broke up, her life would fall apart.

She'd send me love letters written in blood.

Maybe she'd even smack me around.

I ransacked every dumpster marked "Disrespectful Cunts."

I finally found her and got what I wanted.

It was definitely overrated.

"I'm having a REALLY bad day today…"

7:45 AM. He'd just woken up and already was spewing negativity. His entire body was shaking. This kind of thing happened all the time, seemingly at random. It didn't matter what happened on any given day; for him, the next moment could always be a nightmare. It was the past getting the best of him, taking control, screaming in his face that progress was impossible, hope a waste of time.

That afternoon, he mauled a female counselor for no reason. Just last week, he revealed during dinner that he'd been hiding nails inside a recent wrist wound. He said there'd been three, but I only saw two, and he wouldn't say where the missing one was.

Next week, he'll move to a facility that allows him to be out in public, alone, for at least a few hours every day. If he can display a predetermined level of progress over the next three months, he'll be allowed to have a regular job and much more freedom—possibly even a full discharge from the facility. But he's a time bomb, and I don't at all support his being set loose in the streets.

Dear Nanna,

Sometimes when I think about you my penis moves ever so slightly. It's completely limp when it happens, and it's not like I'm thinking about you in a sexual way. I also know you never molested me. I think it happens because I suffered a form of covert incest. Look it up—it perfectly describes what you did to me. Even now you rarely treat me in an age-appropriate manner, and for years you've acted, at times, like I'm your boyfriend or husband. It's usually when you get angry. You start arguing with me and throwing a fit and calling me names as if we're in a dysfunctional high school relationship. You think you're a good grandmother because you love us and do your best, but I disagree; by that definition, almost every parent in the world is a good parent, and that's obviously not true. Both you and Grandpa were abusive. You didn't adequately take care of us or teach us how to take care of ourselves. You guys used us to try to make your lives better, all the while causing serious, irreparable damage. I know you did your best, but I don't think I can be around you anymore.

Sincerely,

The middle child

P.S. I'm a victim. Don't you ever forget it. I say I want to move on with my life, but I'm lying. I love being a victim.

When she was 12, her younger brother broke her necklace by mistake. Her violent father intervened.

"This time, *you* need to teach him a lesson. He never learns."

She just sat there.

"Slap him, you stupid shit."

She began whacking the 6-year-old's left ear.

"Harder! This ain't a massage!"

The boy passed out and had to be taken to the emergency room, but her father wouldn't let her tag along.

"You have a big mouth. Just like your cunt mother."

As she recounted the story to me, I was overcome by a strong desire to murder the man. Sadly, I never got the chance. My loss, my regret.

"I always wonder why someone hasn't raised a child to be a personal sex slave. Adopted, blood, it don't matter. I mean, I've read about people who had sex with their adopted children, but I'm talking about raising one from birth with the sole purpose of eventually using all their holes and limbs to do my bidding. I'd have to wait until the time is right, you know? I'm not some filthy pedophile. When there's grass on the field, play ball. Everything from the child's diet and exercise habits to its tan lines and hair color could be controlled. I've searched high and low for a gal with blond pubes, but I think that's only in magazines. This would obviously be my chance to make it a reality. A custom-made bitch. Haha. I like the sound of that. Much better than all these dumb sluts with their attitudes and rudeness and snobbiness and 'self-respect.' You think you're so hot, don't you? You wear tight clothes so everyone will stare at you, and then you pull that 'he's sexually harassing me' bullshit? This country wants to legislate every god-damn thing. Let's let people be people for once. Men can be men and women can be women. Every woman loves rough sex, anyway. It's always, 'Harder! Harder! Fuck me harder!' Yeah I know, sometimes their vaginas are sensitive because they have a cottage-cheesy yeast infection and they ask you to go a little slower. But every woman *wants* to be fucked harder and fucked more and fucked fucked fucked."

Nerve damage caused her to urinate and defecate on herself several times a day. It also made her very overweight. She was 14. A fat 14-year-old girl who stunk of piss and shit. A fat 14-year-old girl who stunk of piss and shit yet had no problem attracting customers who'd pay twenty dollars for a blow job. She had a great outlook on life for an overweight early teen accustomed to being ensconced in excrement and raped by customers and boyfriends. I bet she has a few kids by now, lucky to have been born into the fertile land that is her life. Look for them soon at your nearest prison or street corner. Be sure to curse whatever dirty whore brought those pieces of trash into the world. Dirty whore she may be, she also has a great sense of humor and the resilience you can only fantasize about having. Or at least she did when I knew her, before she became just another dirty whore.

From the second I wake up, my mind's racing, usually with negative, critical, angry thoughts. They continue until I fall asleep, and then I can't sleep because my grinding teeth wake me up. I need to find new enemies wherever I am, wherever I go. I always find a place between myself and at least one other person to draw a line, a boundary, something that separates us. At first, anger crushed me. Then it helped me while crushing me. Now I just don't want it anymore. I'd offer it to you, but there's no way you could handle this load. I hold grudges better than you, I get revenge better than you, I hate better than you, I embrace my anger better than you. And now it's killing me. Who am I without my anger? I'm no one. I see that now. Help me.

Sexual predator.

She's not allowed to have roommates like the other
kids do.

A motion detector in her room alerts the counselors
if she gets off her bed at night.

Tomorrow's her 11th birthday.

During the week he lived with his father and on weekends with his mother. Every Monday, he'd describe to daddy all the viciousness mommy had perpetrated upon his young body: the kicking, the punching, the scratching…

"I'll take care of it."

This conversation took place hundreds of times. Years passed, nothing changed. It only got worse.

When he was 13, he pressed his father to explain his inaction on the whole, you know, abuse thing. Why nothing had changed. The man admitted to his son that because the mother knew about his part-time drug dealing, she could retaliate against any legal action he initiated by reporting him to the police.

"And I could lose my whole dental practice."

I feel like I see life clearly. I'm in a difficult transition period, but I know I'm exactly where I need to be. I've seen the writing on the wall and what the future holds for me if I don't change. I'm so sick of not being present—*here, now*, in the *moment*. The years seem to be over before they even begin, and the feeling that time used to pass slower continuously intensifies. I can't take it anymore. Time didn't go by slower when I was younger because I had less cares, less stress, and less responsibility; it was because no matter what I was doing, that's what I was doing—I was *there, present*. Of course I remembered the past and thought about the future, but it was different. It wasn't mourning, romanticizing, yearning for, or getting angry about the past. And thinking about the future wasn't turning so many moments and decisions and periods into preparation for something that never comes. I wasn't locked into my debt or bad experiences. I was present and in the moment, whether I was crying or laughing.

I'm so fed up with this lifestyle, one where it feels like no matter what I do, I'm stuck with certain things that get me down or worried or stressed. I need to relearn how to be present, how to not waste so much time in my mind, how to not let my negative thoughts control me. It seems like the people deemed the healthiest are those who use their stress to better themselves, those with the safest, cleanest forms of escapism. But while jogging might be a more productive and positive outlet than getting drunk, you still need to deal with life once the activity's finished. And I aspire to a life I don't want to escape from.

I want to unplug myself from all my bad habits, everything from my destructive criticism to my negative trains of thoughts that waste time and energy. I finally recognize these habits for what they really are: addictions—addictions that still get the best of me way too often. I need to be better to myself. I love being alive; I know it and I feel it. But I need to *be* it.

You ran away from the facility and got raped at a club. It wasn't the first time you'd been raped. Six months later, you ran away again and again got raped. Probably not how you envisioned celebrating your 15th birthday. Now you're expected to pull your life together and become a productive, healthy member of society. I wish you stood better odds.

My friends and I gathered around a dead squirrel lying on the side of the road. One of the guys picked up a brick and dropped it on the carcass; it bounced off and guts spilled out of the torso. He kept doing it over and over. I couldn't bear to look anymore—cruelty to animals was wrong, even dead ones. Despite hearing such objections in my head, I didn't say a word.

Three years later I started to frequently beat my dog. Many more years would pass before I started speaking my mind.

There was one boy who only spent about a month in the facility before losing control and going on one of the worst runs of violence the place had ever seen, brutalizing counselor after counselor before one finally pressed charges.*

Any counselor who pressed charges against one of the kids was to expect vilification and condemnation from virtually the entire facility; doing so was considered a flagrant betrayal of the organization's motto/policy ("unconditional love") and what the counselors had signed on to deal with and accept: physical, verbal, and sometimes sexual abuse. Most counselors had no idea they were allowed to call the police on one of the residents; the organization went out of its way to conceal this right.

One of his encores was luring a therapist into his room by asking for help folding laundry. Within seconds he connected with six punches to her nose, splattering blood on the walls. Other counselors hurried to aid their co-worker, and during the hour-long restraint that ensued, the boy tried to incite the other residents to cause a riot. Pinned flat on the floor, arms at a right angle to his torso and legs spread a couple feet apart, he looked like an immobile, rabid snow angel.**

**This method of holding the residents was a strategy designed to prevent them from being able to muster anything close to their maximum strength, while simultaneously meeting third party standards*

for the safest way to restrain a child on the floor.
Face down was preferred, usually with one staff
member on each limb.

He'd obliterated the therapist's nose, requiring
her to take a break from saving the world for a few
days. This was the fourth time she'd been assaulted
and it wouldn't be the last, yet she always handled
the attacks with dignity and poise.

Two years later, while encouraging an agitated
resident to sit quietly during class, another kid
stood up and kicked her in the stomach. Four counselors ran to help, and after some flailing and
kicking, each was able to seize one of the teenager's
limbs. They carried him to the seclusion room to a
soundtrack of threats and insults and variations of
"fuck your mother."

One veteran counselor reached his breaking
point, repeating over and over that he was done,
that he couldn't take it anymore, that he'd had
enough of the violence. He couldn't speak prop-
erly, like he wanted to bawl but was overcome with
so much rage and disgust that the best he could do
was put forth pitiful, barely audible, weepy com-
plaints and promises that he was done done done,
that he would finish out the shift and never return.
He'd worked there for so long and kept ranting
and ranting, not just to convince his co-workers he
was leaving, but to convince *himself*, as if he re-
quired witnesses to hold him to his word and
would otherwise never leave because he was too
scared to find another job, too scared to say

goodbye to a place that—despite how many nightmares it generated—at least provided some fulfillment and sense of camaraderie.

It's not easy to be optimistic and hopeful after you come to know and love some of the young victims of sexual abuse, violence, poverty, neglect, drugs, and rape. It's taking me a while to climb out of this hatred, this noxious cynicism. I'm doing my best.

Your grandfather fathered you.

Hip hop's your favorite kind of music.

You tried to kill yourself last night, but failed.

In seven months, you'll succeed.

My friend and I listened to ABBA on the way to the funeral.

We were trying to celebrate your existence.

I feel privileged to have spent so much time guarding you while you slept.

You were an amazing person.

I still remember the last time I saw you alive.

I wish I'd been able to ignore the facility's rules about physical contact between counselors and residents.

Then I could have reciprocated your attempt at a real goodbye hug.

I've replayed it in my head so many times.

I'm convinced you knew your life would be over soon and that we'd never see each other again.

I wish I'd hugged you a little tighter.